Journey

OTHER YEARLING BOOKS YOU WILL ENJOY:

BABY, *Patricia MacLachlan*

ISLAND OF THE BLUE DOLPHINS, *Scott O'Dell*

ZIA, *Scott O'Dell*

MY NAME IS NOT ANGELICA, *Scott O'Dell*

CALICO CAPTIVE, *Elizabeth George Speare*

THE SIGN OF THE BEAVER, *Elizabeth George Speare*

THE WITCH OF BLACKBIRD POND, *Elizabeth George Speare*

THE VOYAGE OF THE FROG, *Gary Paulsen*

THE WINTER ROOM, *Gary Paulsen*

THE MONUMENT, *Gary Paulsen*

YEARLING BOOKS are designed especially to entertain and enlighten young people. Patricia Reilly Giff, consultant to this series, received her bachelor's degree from Marymount College and a master's degree in history from St. John's University. She holds a Professional Diploma in Reading and a Doctorate of Humane Letters from Hofstra University. She was a teacher and reading consultant for many years, and is the author of numerous books for young readers.

For a complete listing of all Yearling titles, write to Dell Readers Service,
P.O. Box 1045,
South Holland, IL 60473.

Patricia MacLachlan

Journey

A YEARLING BOOK

Published by
Bantam Doubleday Dell Books for Young Readers
a division of
Bantam Doubleday Dell Publishing Group, Inc.
1540 Broadway
New York, New York 10036

The trademarks Yearling® and Dell® are registered in the U.S. Patent and
Trademark Office and in other countries.

ISBN: 0-440-40809-1

Reprinted by arrangement with Delacorte Press

Printed in the United States of America

September 1993

15 14 13 12 11

FOR JOHN MACLACHLAN

It is our inward journey that leads us through time—forward or back, seldom in a straight line, most often spiraling.

—Eudora Welty,
ONE WRITER'S BEGINNINGS

Photography is a tool for dealing with things everybody knows about but isn't attending to.

—Emmet Gowin, in
ON PHOTOGRAPHY,
by Susan Sontag

Mama named me Journey. Journey, as if somehow she wished her restlessness on me. But it was Mama who would be gone the year that I was eleven—before spring crashed onto our hillside with explosions of mountain laurel, before summer came with the soft slap of the screen door, breathless nights, and mildew on the books. I should have known, but I didn't. My older sister Cat knew. Grandma knew, but Grandma kept it to herself. Grandfather knew and said so.

Mama stood in the barn, her suitcase at her feet.

"I'll send money," she said. "For Cat and Journey."

"That's not good enough, Liddie," said Grandfather.

"I'll be back, Journey," my mother said softly.

But I looked up and saw the way the light trembled in her hair, making her look like an angel, someone not earthbound. Even in that moment she was gone.

"No, son," Grandfather said to me, his voice loud in the barn. "She won't be back."

And that was when I hit him.

Chapter One

MY GRANDFATHER is belly down in the meadow with his camera, taking a close-up of a cow pie. He has, in the weeks since Mama left, taken many photographs—one of our least trustworthy cow, Mary Louise, standing up to her hocks in meadow muck; one of my grandmother in the pantry, reading a book while bees, drawn to her currant wine, surround her head in a small halo; and many of himself, taken with the self-timer device he's not yet figured out. The pictures of himself fascinate him. They line the back of the barn wall in a series of my grandfather in flight, dressed in overalls, caught in the moment of entering the picture, or leaving it; some with grand dimwitted smiles, his hair flying; one of a long, work-worn hand stretched out gracefully, the only part of him able to make it into the frame before the camera clicks.

Cat gave him the camera in one of her fits of cleanliness.

"I've given up the camera," she yelled, her head underneath the bed, unearthing her life. "I've given up the flute and most everything else. Including meat," she said pointedly. "I have spent the entire afternoon looking into the eyes of a cow, and have become a vegetarian."

"Which cow?" asked my grandmother, not kidding.

Cat gave her a quick look. Grandfather picked up Cat's camera and peered through the lens.

"You tired of this, Cat?"

Cat sighed.

"My pictures are so . . ." She waved her hand to the pile of pictures. "So . . ."

"Boring," Grandfather finished for her.

I felt my face flush with anger, but Cat laughed.

"Take it, Grandpa," she said cheerfully.

Grandfather turned to me.

"Journey?"

"No."

What did he think I'd take pictures of? This farm? I could close my eyes and see it—the spruce trees at the edge of the meadow, the stream cutting through, the stone walls that framed it all. I knew every inch of every acre. What would pictures tell me? And the people. What would pictures tell me of my grand-mother, so secretive; my grandfather, tall and blunt?

On Cat's dresser was a picture of our father who had gone away somewhere a long time ago. He was young in the picture, laughing, his eyes looking past the camera, past the place, past me. When I was little, I carried that picture around, trying to remember him, trying to place the picture so that the eyes would look into mine. But they never did. His face was like carved stone, not flesh and blood. And the picture never told me the things I wanted to know.

Did he think about Cat and me? Where was he? Would I know him if I saw him?

I turned and the camera clicked: Grandfather's first picture of me. I stared at him angrily, and slowly he lowered the camera and looked at me with a surprised and dismayed expression, as if he'd seen something through the lens that he hadn't expected.

Grandma's voice broke the silence.

"I'll take the flute, Cat. And this."

Grandma had put on the sweatshirt that Mama had given Cat, LIDDIE written across the front in big letters.

"No!" My voice sounded harsher than I meant. "That's Mama's shirt!"

Grandfather put his hand on my shoulder.

"Your mama left it, Journey."

I shook off his hand and stepped away from him.

Grandma stood in the light of the window, her hair all tumbled like Mama's in the barn. I looked at Cat to see if she noticed, but Cat was smiling at Grandma.

"You look wonderful, Gran."

Cat pulled me after her and went to hug

Grandma. And Grandfather took a picture that
would startle me every time I saw it: not
Grandma, her hair tied back with a piece of
string, smiling slightly as if she knew the secrets
of the world; not Cat, her head thrown back,
laughing; but my face, staring into the camera
with such fury that even in the midst of the light
and the laughter the focus of the picture is me.

Chapter Two

The first letter that wasn't a letter came in the
noon mail. It lay in the middle of the kitchen
table like a dropped apple, addressed to Cat and
me, Mama's name in the left-hand corner.

I'd watched Cat walk up the front path from
the mailbox, slowly, as if caught by the camera
in slow motion or in a series of what Grandfather called stills: Cat smiling. Cat looking eager. Cat, her face suddenly unfolding out of a
smile. She brushed past me at the front door and
opened her hand, the letter falling to the table.

"No return address," she said flatly.

My grandmother stirred soup on the stove and looked sideways at me. After a moment she looked away again.

Grandfather, cleaning his camera lens with lens paper, lifted his shoulders in a sigh, the way he always did when he was about to say something I didn't want to hear.

"I expect—" he began.

Grandma's voice made me jump.

"Marcus!" Then softer. "Let it be."

Cat began to cut carrots at the kitchen counter. My grandfather flinched with each violent stroke.

"I think (thwack) that what Grandpa (thwack) means is that there will be (thwack) money in that envelope. Not words."

Cat stopped and stared down at the counter, the sudden silence like noise filling the room.

"Not the words you want," Cat said softly.

I felt tears behind my eyes. There was something soft and sad in Cat's voice that made me think of Mama.

Grandma stopped stirring the soup, and Grandfather cleared his throat.

"You will be disappointed," he said.

"I'm not disappointed," I said loudly. "I'm not!"

I reached over and tore off one end of the envelope, blowing inside the way Grandfather always did.

Inside were two small packets of money, the bills fastened with paper clips and a torn piece of paper on each. One said CAT. The other said JOURNEY. The paper clip over my name was bent, as if Mama might have tried to make it right and hadn't. I stared at that paper clip for a long time.

"There are words," I said. My voice rose. "There are words! Our names are there. Our names are words!"

There was silence. The sound of my voice hung in the air between us. Cat turned to face me.

"Journey, you keep the money. Do whatever you want with it."

She began to cut the carrots again, this time calm and steady.

"I'll put it in the bank," I said. Grandma

smiled at me from the stove. Grandfather peered at her through his camera and snapped a picture. I stood, suddenly angry, wanting him to stop taking pictures.

"I'll start a travel account!" I shouted.

Surprised, Grandfather put down his camera.

"So that when Mama tells us where she is, Cat and I can go visit! We'll take a bus . . . or a train. Something fast."

I looked down at the letter in my hand.

"She forgot the return address," I said.

Cat turned at the counter to stare at me.

"She forgot, that's all," I said softly.

Grandma wiped her hands on her apron and came over and put her arms around me. I smelled onion and something like flowers, lilacs maybe, and I burst into tears.

"Ah, Journey," Grandma murmured.

I heard the click of Grandfather's camera.

"Why does he do that?" I asked, my voice muffled in Grandma's shoulder. I leaned back to look at Grandfather. "Why do you do that? Why?"

"Because he needs to," said Grandma softly.

"I don't understand."

"I know," she whispered.

* * *

My bedroom was sun-dappled and quiet, the smell of lilacs strong through the open window, mingling with the lily-of-the-valley from under the bush outside.

"Journey?"

The door opened and Grandma stood there with a bowl of soup in one hand, an album in the other. She set the bowl on the table by my bed. Then she opened the album. It was full of pictures, pictures of people I didn't know— men in black suits and white starched shirts and broad-brimmed hats, women in flowered dresses, and children with bows as big as balloons in their hair. Grandma pointed.

"Me," she said, "when I was Cat's age."

In the picture Grandma sat in the garden swing, looking straight at the camera with a great smile on her face. Tables were set up in the garden with food and pitchers and bowls of flowers.

"This was taken on a long-ago Fourth of July." Grandma closed her eyes. "Nineteen thirty, I think. The day I met your grandfather."

"You look happy," I said.

Grandma nodded and looked at the picture.

"The camera knows," she said.

"The camera knows what?"

She turned more pages.

"And here is your mother, same age, same day, but many years later. Grandpa took that picture. He didn't have so fine a camera as now, of course."

In the picture the girl who was my mama sat behind a table, her face in her hands, looking far off in the distance. All around her were people laughing, talking. Lancie, Mama's sister, made a face at the camera. Uncle Minor, his hair all sunbleached, was caught by the camera taking a handful of cookies. In the background a dog leaped into the air to grab a ball, his ears floating out as if uplifted and held there by the wind. But my mother looked silent and unhearing.

"It's a nice picture," I said. "Except for Mama. It must have been the camera," I said after a moment.

Grandma sighed and took my hand.

"No, it wasn't the camera, Journey. It was your mama. Your mama always wished to be somewhere else."

"Well, now she is," I said.

After a while Grandma got up and left the room. I sat there for a long time, staring at Mama's picture, as if I could will her to turn and talk to the person next to her. If I looked at the picture long enough, my mama would move, stretch, smile at my grandfather behind the camera. But she didn't. I turned away, but her face stayed with me. The expression on Mama's face was one I knew. One I remembered.

Somewhere else. I am very little, five or six, and in overalls and new yellow rubber boots. I follow Mama across the meadow. It has rained and everything is washed and shiny, the sky clear. As I walk my feet make squishing sounds, and when I try to catch up with Mama I fall into the brook. I am not afraid, but when I look up Mama has walked away. Arms pick me up, someone else's arms. Someone else takes off my boots and pours out the water. My grandfather. I am angry. It is not my grandfather I want. It is Mama. But Mama is far ahead, and she doesn't look back. She is somewhere else.

I walked to the window. Birds still sang, flowers still bloomed, cows still slept in the meadow, and I ate soup—now cold—as if my mama hadn't ever gone.

Chapter Three

Cooper appeared, as he always did, through my bedroom window, this time carrying his baby brother close to his chest in a sling, like a chimpanzee carrying its young. Cooper's face was round and smooth, his brown hair cut even around his face as if his mother might have placed an aluminum bowl over his head. Cooper's face grew even fatter with love when he saw my sister. Cat, sitting on my bed, looking through the photograph album, smiled back at

Cooper. She liked him even though he was *my* best friend. She liked him even though he was, in my grandfather's words, "besotted" with her. Almost every year since he was six Cooper had proposed marriage to my sister.

"So?" Cooper raised his eyebrows at me.

I shook my head. Cooper knew that Mama had gone, but he wouldn't ask questions. Questions like Where is she? Why hasn't she written a letter? Why did she go? *Who's to blame here?*

I looked up, startled at my own thought, half afraid I'd spoken out loud, but Cat and Cooper were looking at the baby.

The baby, Emmett, reached his small hand out to Cat, the movement jerky, as if his head wasn't telling his hand how. Cat, smiling, put out her finger, and the baby took it, a sudden contented look settling like silk over his face.

Cooper smiled down at Emmett.

"I've got him for a whole hour while Mama weeds the garden," he said, happily untangling Emmett from the sling. "To shape or ruin his lima-bean brain. What shall it be?"

Emmett leaned back against Cooper and stared at me, as if waiting for an answer, his eyes all dark-wet and wise, and so direct that after a moment I looked away.

"He looks like you, Cooper," said Cat.

"We all look alike," said Cooper. "The whole family, down through the ages, over prairie and sea, desert and mountain. You could toss all our pictures up in the air, and when they came down they'd *all* look like me."

Cat laughed and the baby laughed, too, making us all laugh.

"Well, I don't look like anyone," I said. "Anyone that I know."

Cat scrambled over the bed to pick up the album, turning the pages. Cooper pointed suddenly.

"Is that you, Cat? In the garden?"

Cat was quiet.

"No," she said slowly, "that's Mama. Mama a long time ago."

"Oh." There was a pause, and Cooper looked at me uncomfortably. "It's just that . . ."

"We look so much the same," finished Cat.

She turned back in the album.

"There. That's who I look like!"

It was Grandma's picture in the garden swing.

With the smile. Very carefully Cat took the picture out of the album and walked to the mirror. She held the picture up in front of her and smiled.

"There. You see?"

Cooper and I stood behind her, the baby grinning at us all in the mirror.

"Yes," said Cooper. "I do."

Cat looked at me, waiting.

"Yes," I said. It was as if we all stood there, taking a strange oath, in front of a girl with light-touched hair and another who looked the same but not the same in the picture and now had gray hair tied back with a string.

"But," I couldn't help adding, "you look like Mama, too."

Cat's smile became set and her eyes narrowed, and then the baby gave a sudden excited leap in Cooper's arms, and Grandfather stood behind us.

"Ah," he said to the baby. "Look who's come for a visit. Hello, Cooper."

Grandfather took the camera from around his neck and handed it to me. He held out his arms, and Emmett went to him happily, grabbing for his glasses. Laughing, Grandfather took off his glasses and held them out for Cooper to take, and in that moment I held the camera up to my eyes to hide my surprise. Without his glasses my grandfather's face changed; sharp places became softer. Through the camera I could see the wrinkles at the corners of his eyes that made his eyes less hard; his face smoothed out. He looked younger. *He looked* . . . without thinking I pressed the button and the shutter clicked. Grandfather looked up.

"I'm sorry," I said. "I didn't mean to do that."

"No, no, Journey." He smiled at me and sat down on the bed with the baby. "You can take all the pictures you want."

Grandfather sat Emmett on his knees and took his hands.

"Trot, trot to Boston;
Trot, trot to Lynn . . ."

Emmett bounced and grinned. I held the camera up to my face, my eyes closed.

> *Trot, trot to Boston;*
> *Trot, trot to Lynn;*
> *Watch out, little boy,*
> *Or you'll fall in.*

*   *   *

We are in the garden, the light slanting through the trees. Tall flowers—hollyhocks—are nearby, blooms against the barn. Up and down I go, my eyes fastened on white buttons against a blue shirt. The smell of summer fills the air, and voices rising and falling, and laughter.

Watch out, little boy,

Or you'll . . .

My eyes go up from the shirt button to the neck.

But there is no face.

". . . fall in!"

Cooper and Cat laughed; my eyes opened, and I looked through the viewfinder at Grandfather and at Emmett falling back between his knees, their faces in identical expressions—eyes wide, mouths in an O. The baby's laughter fell like sunlight across the room, and as I pressed the button I wished for a way to save that sound, too.

And then Grandfather stood up and put on his glasses again. Slowly I lowered the camera. The baby crawled on the floor. Cat was turning the pages of the photograph album. Cooper yawned. Everything had changed.

Grandfather ran his fingers through his hair,

looking over my head into the mirror behind me. I turned and our eyes met. I frowned and he frowned, imitating me, but I wouldn't smile. I took the camera from around my neck and handed it to him.

"Things don't look the same through the camera," I said. "Not the way they are in real life."

Putting the camera strap around his neck, he paused, then straightened.

"Sometimes." He tilted his head to one side and spoke to himself in the mirror. "And sometimes pictures show us what is really there."

"How? How can that be?" I asked.

Grandfather lifted his shoulders in a familiar way, then said something unlike him.

"I don't know, Journey. Maybe that is why people take pictures. To see what is there."

Cat shut the photograph album with a snap, like an exclamation point at the end of a sentence. Emmett on the floor began to fuss, and I bent down to pick him up. He looked at me closely, then with a sigh he put his arms around my neck and lay his head down. My heart seemed to beat faster with the feel of it.

"What do you mean, 'to see what is there'?" I asked after a moment, but when I turned around, Grandfather had gone.

"What does he mean?" I asked Cat.

She didn't answer. Instead, she handed me a photograph. It was old, very old and grainy, as if taken through water or sand or wind. In the picture there was a boy holding the reins of a horse. Plowed fields spread out behind him, furrows as straight as train tracks. The horse nuzzled the boy's pocket, as if there might be sugar cubes there, or an apple; but the boy stared into the camera with a face so familiar that I caught my breath.

"Boy," said Cooper beside me, "that could be you, Journey."

"Eee," said Emmett, echoing Cooper.

"Is that a picture of Papa?" I asked Cat.

Cooper snorted.

"Even I know who that is."

Emmett, stirring in my arms, turned to stare at me as if he knew, too.

"Two of a kind," said Cat.

I saw the face in that picture every day in the

mirror. And I had just seen that face through the camera.

The picture was of my grandfather.

Chapter Four

It is late June, the longest day of the year, Grandma tells me, and the hottest so far. Grandfather and I argue all the way to the car. Actually, Grandfather calls it a "dialogue" we're having. I call it a fight. We fight because he wants me to drive to town.

"I don't know how," I tell him loudly, following him to the driveway.

"You'll learn."

"I don't want to learn."

"You'll be glad someday."

"Why?"

"I'm an old man. If I die in back of the wheel one day you can drive."

My sister, surrounded by books in the backseat in case she gets bored, laughs.

I throw her a look that makes her laugh
more.

"I'm only a little boy," I plead.

"Then drive like a little boy," says Grandfather.

The subject is closed, but not before Grandfather tries to take another family picture. In the
distance waves of shimmery heat rise off the
fields, but Grandfather doesn't care. He sets his
camera on a fence post and places us by his car.
He makes Grandma come out of the house to
pretend she is going to town too.

"Get a hat, Lottie," he calls to her.

Grandma puts on her straw hat with the
cloth strawberries and grumbles all the way
down the path to the car.

"Look fetching, Lottie," he tells Grandma as
he leans down to peer through the camera.

"I'm not an actress, Marcus," says Grandma
sharply. "I am a hot, old woman."

"You are a fetching hot, old woman," says
Grandfather, making Grandma laugh.

Beside me, Cat wipes the sweat off her forehead. Grandfather's car is already hot; the black surface gleams in the sun.

"Why are we doing this?" I ask loudly.

"The timer is set!" calls Grandfather, ignoring me. "Ready? Ten . . . nine . . . eight . . ."

"Why?" I ask Cat, my teeth clenched.

Cat elbows me gently, and we watch Grandfather begin to run to the car. Grandma licks her lips.

"Four," chants Grandfather, standing tall and trying, I know, to look stately.

"Three," we all say together, our smiles set.

Above us is the droning noise of a small airplane.

"Don't look up!" yells Grandfather, but he does, and we can't help looking, too.

Not one of us hears the soft whirring sound of the shutter clicking.

*　　　*　　　*

"Oh, Marcus," said Grandma, "it's just . . ." She stopped.

"Lottie," said Grandfather, his lips tight. "I love you dearly, and we've been married for what seems like a hundred and fifty years, but you know there is no such thing as 'just a picture.' "

They looked at each other, and Grandma touched his arm.

"I know," she said.

"Take another," I said, hoping he would forget teaching me to drive the car. "I'm really sorry," I added, and when I said it I realized that I *was* sorry.

Grandfather waved his hand.

"Never mind. Let's get going. I've got rolls of film to drop off and pictures to pick up. I've got things to get in town."

"Things?" asked Grandma. "What things?"

"Things," said Grandfather, moving toward the car. "Photo things. Come on, Journey. Drive."

*   *   *

Grandfather gets in the passenger seat and waits as I climb behind the wheel. There are no seat belts because Grandfather's car is so old. It has scratchy seats and huge fenders. It has a running board. I have never seen another car like his car. My sister says they are extinct. Grandma calls it the passenger pigeon.

I start the car. I know about the clutch and the brake because I can drive a tractor. But Grandfather's car is different, and we lurch off, Grandfather bracing himself with one hand, hanging on to the roof strap with the other, Cat laughing in the backseat.

The moment we get out of sight of the farm my grandfather takes out his camera and hangs out the window, and suddenly I know that he wants me to drive so he can take pictures as we move. I know that if we are in a car crash, Grandfather will photograph it as it happens.

"Keep it steady," says Grandfather, and we pass Millie Bender's parents' fruit stand. Out of the corner of my eye I see a blur of watermelon and peaches, strawberries and Mrs. Bender sitting under a striped umbrella.

We pass a cornfield filled with crows.

"Hey!" yells Grandfather, and the crows rise up in a flapping of wings above us. He leans out backward and aims the camera to the sky.

I laugh.

"Look!" I cry, suddenly excited.

Cooper rides toward us, recognizing the car. He stares at it, about to raise his arm in a wave, when he sees it's me driving. His jaw drops.

"Quick!" I shout. "Take the picture!"

Grandfather leans over me, and he snaps the picture just as Cooper's bicycle begins to wobble. I look in the rearview mirror and watch Cooper watching us.

"You know," I say after a moment, "I bet the picture of us all looking up at the airplane will be fine."

Grandfather looks at me.

"I think you're right, Journey," he says.

"Two of a kind," says Cat.

Chapter Five

Summer rains came, soft at first, with mists that lay like lace over the meadows. When the sky grew darker and the rain steady, Grandma sent us out to gather peonies. Grumbling, we carried dripping pink and white armfuls into the house, filling all the pitchers we could find and a wash- tub in the kitchen. The smell filled the house, and so did the ants that crawled down from the blooms, crisscrossing the house like sightseers.

Grandfather, restless, lurked through the hallways, taking pictures with the new flash attachment bought in town and breaking into sudden dances of ant-stomping. Blasts of light popped everywhere until Grandma ran out of patience.

"I have spots in front of my eyes, Marcus! I can't read! Go away. Be a farmer."

Grandfather was insulted.

"I am a farmer who takes pictures," he said haughtily. Then he brightened. "I am a photographer-farmer."

Grandma, only a little amused, banished him to the barn, where I watched him take cow close-ups until the cows, bothered by the lights, showed him their backsides.

"Maybe the chickens," he muttered.

I stood behind Grandfather, trying to see what he saw through the camera. Then I walked to the back of the barn where his pictures hung,

looking again at the familiar ones of Grandma
and Cat and me. There were new ones, too—
Grandma smiling from the stove, and one of
Cat hoeing in the garden with a fierce look, the
hoe poised above the soil as if she might be
killing a black snake. And then I saw it—the
picture I had taken of Grandfather with Emmett
on his knees, Emmett's mouth opened, light
from the window around them both. The edges
were blurred and soft, as if it were a painting. Or
a memory. *Trot, trot to Boston*. For a moment I
felt like I was Emmett, sitting on someone's
knees. Someone who sang to me. I stared, goose
bumps coming up on my arms. I stepped back to
bend down to see the picture better and bumped
up against Grandfather standing behind me.

"You moved the camera," he said. "That's
why the edges are fuzzy."

I nodded.

"It's not a good picture, I guess."

"Journey," said Grandfather, his voice soft,
"it is a wonderful picture."

"But I moved the camera."

"You did. See how it looks like Emmett and I
are the only ones there, how we look like we're

wrapped in a cocoon, away from the rest of the
world? See how the edges frame us?"

Grandfather's voice rose with excitement,
and I smiled even though I didn't want to.

"Well," I said, embarrassed and pleased.
"Well, it's not perfect."

"Perfect!" Grandfather almost spit out the
word. His face softened. "What is perfect? Journey, a thing doesn't have to be perfect to be fine.
That goes for a picture. That goes for life." He
paused. "Things can be good enough."

I stared at Grandfather, then at my picture.
After a moment I felt Grandfather move behind
me.

"Grandfather?"

"Yes, Journey."

I turned. Grandfather was standing at the
door of the barn, rain pouring off the roof behind him. His old dark green poncho floated
from his shoulders like a king's cape.

I swallowed hard.

"Do you think that Mama left because things
weren't good enough? Do you think that *I*
wasn't . . ."

"No!" Grandfather spoke loudly, his eyes

dark. "No," he said, softer. He made a move
toward me, then stopped. "Do you know that I
tell you the truth? Even when you don't want to
hear it?"

I nodded.

"Which? Yes that I tell you the truth or yes
that you don't want to hear it?"

I was silent, suddenly remembering that
once in this barn he had told me that Mama
would not come back. That was not true. I knew
that was not true. "Sometimes," I said softly.
"Sometimes you tell me the truth."

Grandfather pursed his lips.

"Well, this is an important truth, Journey. It
is not . . ." His voice grew louder. "It—is—
not—your—fault."

There was a pause, then slowly his face
changed, and I knew somehow that we were
thinking the same thing. But of course Grandfather said it.

"You need someone to blame, Journey? Is
that it?"

I backed up a step.

"Well, it's not Mama's fault," I said stub-
bornly.

Grandfather sighed.

"No, I can see that you can't blame Liddie. But that's all right. That's all right."

We stared at each other for a moment; then I turned to look at the picture of him and Emmett again.

"I remember things," I said. "I remember 'Trot, trot to Boston.'" I turned to look at him. "I do."

Grandfather smiled faintly.

"I'm not surprised you remember. But you were very little. You wanted to hear that rhyme over and over and over." His voice trailed off.

I picked up Grandfather's camera and looked at him through the viewfinder, standing there with his poncho and rain hat.

"I remember," I said, snapping the picture just before Grandfather's smile faded, "that I sat on my papa's lap. I remember the button on his shirt. And he sang to me and held my hands. And he wouldn't let me fall. He and Mama kept me safe and took care of me until . . ."

I put the camera down and stared at it.

Until you made them go away.

The words were unspoken, but when I

looked up again, I might just as well have said
them out loud by the look on Grandfather's
face.

"Where are the pictures?" I asked.

"What?" asked Grandfather. "What pictures?"

"The pictures of Papa and Mama and me.
And Cat. When we were babies like Emmett?
When I was on Papa's knees?"

Grandfather looked down at the floor.

"There weren't many," he said.

"I don't need many."

Grandfather sighed.

"They're gone," he said.

Gone.

"You mean Mama took them?" I asked.

Grandfather took a deep breath and looked
me in the eye.

"The truth?"

My skin prickled.

"Yes. Did she take them?"

"No, Journey," said Grandfather. "Your
mama tore them up."

Chapter Six

"I don't believe you're sick," says Cat, standing over my bed like an umpire over home plate. "And if you are sick, you're glad of it. You like us to bring you soup and ginger ale."

"I have a sore throat," I tell her, pulling the covers under my chin.

"Let's see," says Cat, trying to pry my mouth open.

I can hear Grandma in the kitchen practicing scales on the flute.

"I have a temperature, too," I say.

"How many blankets do you have here? One, two, three, a quilt, a bedspread. Journey, you've got five blankets, and it's summer! You may turn into a butterfly."

"Cat, Mama tore up our pictures."

"Yes."

"You knew? Why am I the last to know anything?"

"You know things, Journey. You just don't
want to believe them. You believe what you
want."

Cat, in a sudden motion, whips my covers
off.

"Cat!"

She lets the window shade snap up, and sun
clatters into the room. I put my hands over my
eyes.

"You're not sick, Journey," says Cat, standing at the window. "You're hiding out."

*　　*　　*

Grandma was surprised to see me dressed.

"Journey, are you feeling better?"

"Cat made me get up."

Grandma smiled. She put her flute on my
bureau.

"Cat is a woman of action. She doesn't believe much in introspection."

"Introspection?"

Grandma sat on my bed.

"What you've been doing in here the past two days. Thinking, mostly about yourself."

I looked up quickly to see if this was an insult, but Grandma was looking out to the garden, where Cat was hoeing between the rows.

"Cat believes that if she keeps busy all the things that bother her will go away," said Grandma.

"Does that work?"

Grandma turned to look at me.

"Not entirely. No more than thinking. But you will notice," she added, "that my garden is twice the size it was last year."

I looked out at the rows of lettuce and radishes, the fernlike tops of carrots. Grandma had turned up more grass this year, and she had even planted corn that stood stomach high to me. We watched Cat finish a row, then stand back, wiping the back of her hand over her forehead. She lifted her shoulders suddenly, then began working again.

Grandma leaned against the window frame and looked out, past Cat in the garden, past the meadows. Her face looked sad. *She misses*

Mama, too. Aunt Lancie and Uncle Minor had moved away, and they visited sometimes. But Mama had stayed on to live with Grandma. Mama and Papa. And Mama was the youngest.

"We all do the best we can, you know," said Grandma. "Your sister and I garden ourselves into madness." She looked at me. "You think yourself into a sore throat." She sighed and gestured toward the barn. "And your grandfather takes pictures."

Grandfather, his camera around his neck, was prowling along the stone wall outside, his eye on Cat. Through the window we could see him say something. We could see Cat turn with a surprised look, like a deer startled in the garden, as Grandfather took her picture.

"Watch now, Journey," Grandma whispered. "That old buzzard is going to take a picture of us."

"How do you know?" I whispered back. "He didn't even look this way."

"Oh yes he did. I saw his eyes roll to the side. I am the smartest woman in this room."

"Why are we whispering?" I whispered.

Grandma began to laugh, and she put her

arm around me. I smiled, and we both looked out. Suddenly Grandfather whirled and aimed his camera at us in the window.

"Such a noodle," said Grandma, laughing as he took our picture. She wiped her eyes with a handkerchief.

"Grandma?"

"What?"

"Why did Mama do it? The pictures?"

Grandma shrugged.

"I can't speak for Liddie. I never could, Journey. And it wouldn't be fair to you if I did."

"Then," I said, "I'll have to ask her when I see her."

Grandma looked at me, a quick look. She reached out to smooth my hair.

"I hope you get to do that, Journey. I really do."

Grandma went to the dresser and picked up her flute.

"He shouldn't have told me," I said suddenly. "Grandfather shouldn't have told me about the pictures."

"But, Journey," Grandma said softly, "you asked him." Grandma paused for a moment to look at the old picture of Mama that leaned

against the dresser.

"Funny, isn't it, how we are sometimes angry at the wrong person."

She gave her head a little shake, as if shaking off a fly, then she went out the door.

"You," I whispered to the picture. "I *could* have a sore throat. I *could* have a temperature."

I leaned my elbows on the dresser and peered into Mama's face.

"Do you hear me?"

Chapter Seven

And then the cat came. After the rains, when Grandfather and I were silent and uneasy with each other, and the lawn grew too long, and June bugs threw themselves against the lamplit screens, I heard the soft thump as the cat jumped up to my sill. The cat stared at me, its face like a pansy, and then, without claws, it lifted a paw and hit the window screen. The tiniest of sounds. Very carefully I lifted the screen, and the cat walked inside, across my desk, and settled on my bed as if it were home. As if the cat were someone come back in disguise. Almost at once the cat slept.

Slowly I backed out of the room, racing to the kitchen.

"Cat?"

Grandma looked up.

"Your sister's not here, Journey. Do you want something?"

No. I knew how Grandma felt about cats.

Behind her, Grandfather was standing, leaning against the counter, stirring coffee.

"No, Grandma, thanks. Good night."

"Good night then," said Grandma, threading a needle in the light.

I looked at Grandfather, and he looked back at me, taking a sip of his coffee, his eyes narrowed against the steam. He turned his head to one side, as if he were getting a different view of me. I lifted my shoulders, took a breath, and beckoned to him, putting a finger to my lips. His eyebrows rose. After a moment he put down his coffee, silently following me down the hallway to my room.

"What is it?" he said at my bedroom door.

"Look," I whispered, pulling his arm. I pointed.

"Oh, my," whispered Grandfather. He smiled. "Look at that, all tuckered out."

Slowly he walked to the bed. The cat stretched, looked up at him, then curled up again.

"Whose cat is it?" asked Grandfather.

I was silent.

Grandfather quickly looked down at me.

"Journey," he warned, "no. You know your grandma is not fond of cats. She loves her birds."

"I love this cat," I said. "He tapped on my window screen. I think he's mine."

"Do not," said Grandfather, whispering fiercely, "do not name this cat."

I knew the family rule. Do not name an animal or you'll have to take care of it. If you name it, it's yours.

"He tapped on my screen and walked right in

and went to sleep," I went on, "just like he lives here. And he does."

I put out my hand and stroked the cat, and he put his paws around my hand, hugging me to him.

"See?" I whispered.

Grandfather bent down.

"There's blood here, Journey. See, a little trail on the floor."

Grandfather ran his hands over the cat, who peered at him through slit eyes.

"Here it is. A little cut on his foot."

Grandfather took out his handkerchief and blotted the cat's left paw. Suddenly the cat reached over and took Grandfather's finger in his teeth. I held my breath as Grandfather and the cat stared at each other. After a moment Grandfather smiled.

"You are something," he said to the cat, and to prove it, the cat let go of his finger, turned over, and went back to sleep.

"What is going on here?"

Grandma's voice made Grandfather jump. The cat didn't move.

"Oh, for heaven's sake, Marcus!"

My sister appeared suddenly behind Grandma. Her face lighted up when she saw the cat.

"Oh!" She turned to me. "Have you named him yet?"

"Marcus!" said Grandma warningly, her lips pressed tightly together.

"Now, Lottie," said Grandfather, "this is an injured animal. We have to be humane here."

"You know how I feel about cats," said Grandma. "And cats are not humane to birds."

"We'll put a bell on him," I said. "Two bells, Grandma! Please!" Grandma's face was stern. I turned to Grandfather. "I need this cat."

My own words startled me, and Grandfather cleared his throat.

"Actually, Lottie, it's unfortunate, I know, but Journey has named him already."

I stared at Grandfather. Grandma saw my surprise.

"Really," she said, folding her arms across her chest. "And what would that name be?"

"Yes," said Grandfather. His eyes roamed the room. "His name is . . ." Grandfather looked at the vase of peonies by the window. "His name is

Bloom, isn't that what you called him, Journey?"

"Yes." I nodded.

"Oh, push," said Grandma, half smiling, "you just made that up, old man. You might just as well have said Peony."

"Lottie," said Grandfather, "Journey knows that Peony is no name for a cat."

The screen opened, and Cooper poked his head in.

"I saw the lights."

He climbed in, closing the screen behind him, and then he saw the cat. Cooper peered at Grandfather, at my sister leaning against the wall, and at Grandma with her arms still folded. Finally he looked at me.

"Of course you named him," he said, making Grandfather's lips twitch.

"Bloom," I said.

"I'll get the camera," said Grandfather.

*   *   *

As it turned out the name Bloom fit the cat well. In Grandma's words, Bloom was about to burst into flower. In Grandfather's words, "He's a she, she's pregnant. You're going to be a papa."

Grandma pretended anger at the idea of more than one cat. But I thought that she'd known the moment she first saw Bloom. And Bloom, if she loved anyone, loved Grandma. She ran to her in the morning with a small, eager sound of welcome. She brought sodden and well-chewed mice to the doorstep, waiting proudly for Grandma to run through all her words of disgust. She sat beside Grandma on the living room couch at night, watching Grandma closely.

We tied a bell on Bloom so she wouldn't catch birds, but Bloom would not wear it, managing to chew it off. Late into the night we heard the sound of Bloom batting it up and down the hallways of the house before she came to my bed to sleep. But as far as I knew, Bloom never caught a bird. If she did, she never brought it to Grandma's doorstep.

"She knows," said Cat admiringly.

"She's the most intelligent cat I've ever known," added Cooper, who had never known any cat well. "Intelligent enough to know your grandma would kill her and toss her on the compost heap."

I knew better. I knew that Grandma and Bloom had a secret life of their own. Once, hidden in the pantry, I heard what Bloom heard each day from Grandma.

"Oh no, you filthy little cannibal! Take that mouse away, you wretch!" Then whispered, "You are one splendid girl. The best in all the world. Would you like a treat?"

One morning I borrowed Grandpa's camera and stalked them in the garden, and I took a picture of Grandma leaning over the onions to whisper to Bloom, Bloom's tail high, her face lifted to Grandma's, almost a kiss.

Days later, when Grandfather saw the picture he grew very quiet, and when I looked up at him his eyes were wet. He pinned the picture on the wall of the barn, and we stood next to each other, not speaking for a long time. Then we had the shortest conversation of our lives so far.

"Lottie needs that cat," said Grandfather.

I nodded.

"The camera knows," I said.

Chapter Eight

The days grew hot and Bloom grew fat. Humid air hung heavy as parlor drapes in the house, but still no letters came—only small packets of money with envelopes leaving a postmark path I couldn't follow. Grandma took the fruit out of her crystal bowl in the dining room, and Bloom climbed in happily to keep cool. Grandfather groused ("She doesn't even let me *wash* that bowl"), but when Grandma left he set the table with all the china and silver, candles burning, and took a picture of Bloom lolling in the bowl like a queen. Then he handed me the camera, and I took a picture of them both—Bloom in the bowl and Grandfather at the head of the table, the candle flames reflected in their eyes.

During the hot days Grandfather was seized by picture taking. He took a picture of Cat and me, up to our necks in the brook, and Cooper, his white wrinkled feet thrust up between our faces. He took Grandma in the hammock under the tulip tree, playing her flute to Bloom, above her on a branch. He made me drive the John Deere through the hayfield as he perched dangerously over the cutter, photographing the blades as they turned.

"If I fall," he yelled over the noise of the engine, "grab the camera!"

And he maddened the chickens, trying to take a still life of eggs in the henhouse.

But it was the family pictures that consumed him and drove us into hiding. We would hear him call "Everyone!" innocently, and we would run to different parts of the house— Grandma into the pantry, closing the door after her, Cat under her bed, and me to the attic. But he always found us. Once, we posed in the doorway of the barn, nicely framed, but a chicken flew past us. Even Bloom caught the tone and would streak past us into the nearest room or behind the curtains. Or, just that once, into Mama's room.

That's why it was Bloom who found them.

Under the bed in the room we never entered, in the room that Mama had stripped of herself, Bloom hid next to the box, waiting for us to find her.

"What is this?" said Cat, lying down next to the bed. "Come out, Bloom."

I lay down, too, lifting the dust ruffle. Bloom batted at my hand, then jumped into a box. I reached out and pulled the box out from under, Bloom crouched down inside.

Behind us was a noise. Grandfather held Grandma's arm as if she were his captive.

"Come on, now, I've caught her. Just one picture."

And then Bloom jumped out of the box.

And Grandfather's face changed.

Inside the box were torn pictures, hundreds of them. Bits and pieces of faces and arms and bodies; slices of scenes, of sky and flowers; a door, a porch here; the barn, the face of a cow peering over the fence. *A baby's hand*.

I stood up. Grandma put her hand on my shoulder.

"She didn't throw them away," I said, my voice a whisper.

"Doesn't look like it," said Grandfather stiffly.

He exchanged a look with Grandma.

"Well," said Cat, getting up and dusting off her pants. "She sure did in our family. Didn't she?"

No one spoke. Then Cat looked up at Grandfather and Grandma. "It looks like murder to me."

Murder. The word washed over me. It did look like a killing. Cat was right. Inside that box were people: Cat and Mama and Papa. And me. Was that baby's hand my hand?

I picked up the box and looked at Cat. Her face was pale. Tears sat at the corners of her eyes.

"I'll fix this, Cat," I said to her. "I'll tape these pictures back together again."

"Oh, Journey," began Grandma.

But Grandfather stopped her.

"It's all right, Lottie. Journey's got a right to these pictures."

He reached into the box and cradled a handful of torn pictures in his hand. Pieces slipped through his fingers like water.

"It's Journey's past," he said.

*   *   *

Morning has come and gone, and afternoon, too. A standing lamp shines down, a yellow pool on the pictures. Faces stare up at me, and a dog I don't remember or I've forgotten, and Cat's face when she was seven or eight. But it is the baby's hand. Where is the face? And where is the picture of the man who holds him?

For a long time I work alone, sorting and shifting picture pieces like a giant puzzle. But I can piece together only a few. Not the ones I want. Cat comes to crouch down, but she only looks. Grandma comes to bring me dinner on a plate, and later Grandfather stands above me so he won't cast a shadow. He leans down for a moment, picking up a piece, then putting it back. Then, without a sound, he is gone.

There is moonlight at the windows when something, a movement in the room, startles me. Bloom walks across the pictures, and I look up and Cooper is sitting in a chair by the window. He is wearing a strange cowboy hat, too small, that sits high on his head. We stare at each other.

"Cooper," I say, my voice soft, "I will put all these pictures back together, and everything will be all right."

Cooper is silent. I look up at him.

"It will," I say. "It will," I whisper.

Chapter Nine

I am dreaming. I always know when I am dreaming because I can fly. I fly over the farm, over the blueberry barren, over the barn and house. I fly over Grandfather in the field, and when I call down to him he raises his camera and takes a picture of me with my wings all warm. Then I fly down a road. The road turns into a map, and the map is large with all the roads marked, and I follow all the towns one by

one by one. When I try to call down again, my
voice has changed to a bird's voice. And no one looks up.

I woke, sweating, with early light coming in the window. I sat up, looking over to the chair in the corner, and then I remembered that Cooper had left, long ago. Long ago, after we had worked, and Cooper had sat back suddenly and told me that it was impossible. That was the word he used, *impossible.* That I couldn't patch all the pictures together because there were so many; more than I had thought. *Look,* he had said to me, *some of these pictures are very old; here is part of your grandmother's face when she was very little. Like the picture in the swing. Remember?*

My grandma's face. *She had even torn up my grandma.*

And I told Cooper his cowboy hat looked stupid.

And he left.

And I knew Mama was never coming back.

I got up and looked out the window. Cooper's bike leaned against the house, and I half expected to see him there, too, but I knew he had walked home alone through the fields in the dark.

Behind me the lamp was still on, its pale yellow light spilling out over the pictures. I bent down and picked up the pieces, trying not to look at the faces of the people as I filled the box and put it in my closet. Bloom appeared to rub her face against my arm. With a small sound, she jumped into the box and lay there, looking up at me through tired eyes.

"The box is yours, Bloom," I said. "You found it, after all."

And I climbed out the window, very quietly so as not to wake anyone, and began to pedal Cooper's bicycle down the road to his house. I didn't get very far when I began to cry.

*   *   *

Cooper's house was white clapboard with a cement sidewalk, his mother's narrow lines of alternating white petunias and red salvia on either side. I thought of Grandma's growing garden of flowers and vegetables, getting larger as the days passed. Cooper's mother didn't like to garden.

"If God had wanted us to garden, he would have had plots all dug up, waiting for us. And he wouldn't have created weeds, either," she once said.

I wheeled the bicycle up the walk. I was not surprised to see Cooper sitting on the front porch in a white metal chair. I was not surprised, either, that he still wore his cowboy hat.

"Thanks for bringing my bike," he said.

"I'm sorry. What I said about your hat," I told him.

Cooper nodded. I sat down next to him.

We looked out over the neat yard.

"You been crying?" asked Cooper, not looking at me.

"Yes."

After a moment Cooper shrugged his shoulders like Grandfather.

"Well, then," he said, "let's go in. Mrs. Mac-Dougal is making breakfast."

Cooper called his mother Mrs. MacDougal. So did Mr. MacDougal. I expected that one day soon Emmett would ask for his bottle please, Mrs. MacDougal.

In the kitchen Cooper's mother was making pancakes. Emmett sat in his high chair, smears of banana and applesauce across his face and up his arms to his elbows. His hair was stuck to his scalp with pancake syrup. Food lined the creases of his neck like putty.

"He's learning to feed himself," explained Mrs. MacDougal, putting a plate in front of me. "You'll have some breakfast, Journey?"

Emmett grinned at me, banana oozing around his two front teeth.

"Just a little, please," I said, and Cooper laughed.

"Mr. MacDougal!" called Cooper's mother.

"I've eaten, Mrs. MacDougal!" answered Cooper's father from upstairs. But soon he exploded into the room in his work clothes and kissed Emmett, then Cooper, then Mrs. MacDougal, then me. I was startled, trying to remember the last time someone had kissed me. The kiss was warm on my forehead, and I bent my head down to finish my pancake.

Cooper's house was filled with Mac-Dougals—pictures on the refrigerator and above the doorway. After we ate I followed Cooper into the dining room, where his great-grandparents hung over the sideboard. In the living room were pictures of Cooper as a baby, plump as a plum; Mr. and Mrs. MacDougal before they were married; and newer pictures of Emmett, all cleaned up and looking wise. I walked from room to room with Cooper, watching his life on the walls.

"Grandfather says pictures show us the truth sometimes," I said.

Mrs. MacDougal stood in the doorway, watching us.

"Sometimes, maybe. But do you see that picture of me, there on the piano?"

I picked up the picture, framed in silver. Mrs. MacDougal was young, her mother and father standing formally behind her, her brothers flanking her protectively.

"Don't we look the perfect family?"

I smiled at her and nodded.

"Well, my brother Fergus, there on the left, was pinching the devil out of me when that picture was taken. He did that all my life. He still does."

I peered at the picture closely, searching for a look that told me this. But there were only smiles.

"Sometimes," said Mrs. MacDougal, "the truth is somewhere behind the pictures. Not in them."

In the kitchen, still in his high chair, Emmett began to fuss.

"Ah, well," said Mrs. MacDougal, "I'd better go hose him down." She turned. "It's early, Journey. Do Marcus and Lottie know where you are?"

"I'm going to ride him home on my bike, Mrs. MacDougal," said Cooper.

*   *   *

We ride up the dirt road, me sitting on the seat, my legs out, Cooper pedaling in front of me. I hold on to his waist, and we pass fields and meadows and cows; we pass Weezer, the Moodys' old dog, who makes a show of chasing us.

"Weezer, Weezer," chants Cooper, and Weezer stops, stunned by the sound of his name, just before he runs into the mailbox.

We pass the Fullers' horse farm, and the foals race along the fence, sending up little dust clouds when they stop. Cooper pedals up the long driveway to my house and right up over the grass to my bedroom window. And when I open the screen and climb in, Cooper behind me, everyone is there: Grandma, Grandfather, and Cat, staring into my closet.

Bloom has had her kittens.

Chapter Ten

In the box of pictures, now ruined, were Bloom and her kittens: four tiny bodies, all wet and dark.

"I've only been gone an hour," I whispered.

Grandma smiled.

"That's all it takes, sometimes."

"Sorry about the pictures, Journey," said Grandfather.

I sighed.

"It's all right. It was impossible. But it was that baby's hand ..." My voice trailed off.

We watched the kittens fumbling to nurse and listened to their soft mewings.

Bloom stared up at Grandma.

"Yes," Grandma said as if answering a question the rest of us hadn't heard, "you are a wonderful mother!"

Cat reached down and rubbed Bloom's chin.

"Who taught her?" I asked suddenly.

"Taught her what?" said Cooper. "How to have kittens?"

"No," I said. "How to be a mother."

There was a silence. Grandfather lifted his shoulders.

"Mothers know," he said, looking at Grandma.

Cat said what I was thinking.

"Not all of them."

No one spoke, but as if Bloom had understood our words, she began to clean her babies, showing us how to be a mother.

"Grandpa," I said, "I want to take a picture. With the timer."

My grandmother and Cat groaned at the same time.

"Oh, no," complained Cat. "Don't tell me, two of them!"

Grandfather grinned at me.

"Of course he wants to take a family picture. Out in the hall, Journey."

In the hallway Grandfather's camera and his tripod leaned against the wall.

"I'll take the picture. I'm not family," Cooper called to me.

I stood in the doorway and looked at Cooper through the viewfinder. His cowboy hat still sat on top of his head.

"Cooper," I said, "you're part of the family. But *I* want to take this picture."

When I moved the camera, I saw Grandfather smiling at me from across the room.

"Now," I said. "Everyone . . ."

There was laughter.

"What?" I asked.

"You sound like you-know-who," said Cat, bending her head toward Grandfather.

"Who?" asked Grandfather.

"The photographer twins," said Cooper wryly.

"Now," I said. "Everybody . . ." I shot a look at Cat.

Grandma sat, Cat next to her, leaning back against her shoulder. Cooper knelt behind them, Grandfather on the other side, watching me closely.

"Ready?" I said.

*   *   *

Time slows somehow as I look through the camera. I watch Bloom look at her babies; I watch Grandma kiss the top of Cat's head and Cat turn to smile up at her; I see Cooper with his dumb hat, and my grandfather, smiling at me because he knows I am looking at him.

Smile, I say to them, but I don't need to say it

because they are all smiling. Real smiles, with their eyes, too. *Ten, nine, eight,* I say, and Cooper's hat tilts and Cat snorts with laughter. *Seven, six.* I run to get into the picture, and Grandfather reaches out a hand toward me. I tumble into his arms, across his lap, and he holds me there, looking a little surprised, as if I'm a newborn baby. I stare at the button on his shirt. Then I stare up at his face. *Quick,* he whispers to me, and I turn and look into the camera just as the shutter clicks and Cooper's hat falls down.

*   *   *

The kitchen was dark and cool and quiet. Cooper had stayed for dinner: chicken and mashed potatoes and peas.

"It's good to eat with people who don't have food on their faces," said Cooper seriously. He paused. "But I love Emmett."

"You do," agreed Grandma.

Grandfather, his chin leaning on his hand, looked at Cooper.

"You're a good brother," he said.

Under the table I felt a sudden brush against my legs. Bloom looked up at me; then she walked to the screen door.

"Where's she going?" I asked, alarmed.

Cat got up from the dinner table.

"She's going out, Journey. Don't fret." She opened the door, and Bloom went out to sit on the porch. Cat turned to look at me. "She'll come back," she said softly.

Cooper got up, too.

"Thank you," he said. "I like to get home for Emmett's bath."

He went out to the porch and stood for a moment next to Bloom. Then he put on his hat.

" 'Bye, Cooper," said Cat.

We went out, all of us, and waved to Cooper.

"Maybe someday," said Cat thoughtfully, "I *will* marry him."

Grandma, smiling, tapped Cat on her shoulder. The two of them went to their garden.

Grandfather stood next to me, fiddling with his camera. I looked up at him, trying hard to remember something new, something at the edge of my mind. He put the camera around his neck.

"Think I'll take a small walk to the hen-house."

I smiled and watched him walk down the steps. Inside, the phone rang, and he turned.

"I'll get it," I called to him.

*   *   *

"Hello."

I look out the screen door.

"Journey, is that you?" says my mother.

There is crackling on the line, and I stand very still, watching my grandfather walk away from the house.

"Journey?" Her voice is stronger now. "So, how have you been?"

I take a breath.

"A cat has come," I say. "And the cat is a very good mother." My voice rises. "And she is staying here with me. Forever."

Chapter Eleven

Grandfather found me in the barn. Light slanted through the windows, and dust motes floated in the air between us. He sat next to me on the bench in front of the wall of pictures. There were dozens now that spread across the back wall, some I'd never seen.

"That's a new one," I said, pointing to a close-up of a fierce-looking chicken.

"That chicken pecked me on the wrist," said Grandfather. He held out his hand to show me the small red puncture wound. "Taking pictures is dangerous business."

I nodded, looking at the picture I had taken, all soft and blurred. My grandfather holding Emmett on his knees.

There was silence.

"She asked me how I was," I said after a

moment. I looked up at Grandfather. "And she
never said she was sorry for leaving."

Grandfather sighed.

"No. Liddie doesn't want to feel guilty."

"Well, she is guilty," I said so softly that
Grandfather bent his head down next to me to
hear. "And then she said, 'They were only pictures, Journey.' "

Grandfather reached over and put his arm
around me. I leaned against him.

"A picture stops a little piece of time, good or
bad, and saves it," he said. "Your mama never
thought there was anything worth looking back
on after your papa left. She thought all good
things were ahead of her, waiting to happen . . .
just around the corner. Your mama doesn't
really understand about the pictures."

"But we understand, don't we," I said.

Grandfather's arm tightened around me.

"We do."

I sighed.

"I sure would like things to look back on."

It was quiet in the barn. Somewhere in the
garden Grandma was playing the flute, the beginnings of a song I didn't know.

"Grandma's getting better," I said.

"Yes," said Grandfather. "And it's a good thing, too," he added, making me smile.

"Mama wants me to visit her," I said.

Grandfather got up and went to the wall of pictures and bent down as if he were examining them.

"I told her I couldn't. I told her I have a cat and kittens to take care of."

Grandfather straightened.

"I told her someday, maybe; if she sent me words instead of money, I might visit. Maybe."

Grandfather said nothing.

"Grandfather?"

"What, Journey?" His voice was soft.

"I told her that nothing is perfect. Sometimes things are good enough."

I got up and stood next to him and looked at the family picture of all of us, our necks all white in the sun as we looked up at the airplane overhead.

"I like that picture," I said.

"So do I. You said it would be a good picture. Remember?"

I looked at the picture of us all framed in the barn doorway, with a blur of chicken flying past.

"Is that the chicken that pecked you?" I asked.

Grandfather began to laugh.

"Might be!"

He threw back his head, and I stared at him, surprised at that sound. It had been a long time since I'd heard him laugh, and suddenly I thought of Mr. MacDougal's kiss on my forehead, how strange it had felt.

I watched Grandfather. And then, before he stopped laughing—because I wanted to remember what it was like—I stood on tiptoe and kissed him.

Chapter Twelve

Two months. Two months and a little more had gone by. It didn't seem so long when you said it, but Grandma said that time was different depending on which journey you were taking—a trip to the mountains or a trip to get your tooth pulled.

"Sometimes things happen quickly before you have a chance to think about them. Like the hummingbird that comes to my bee balm in the garden," said Grandma. "You don't see him come, and you hardly see him go."

Like Mama's leaving.

Two months. The kittens had grown what seemed half a lifetime in that time, staggering around the house, leaping straight up in the air when they came on Grandfather's boots. Emmett was learning words like "Mama" and "Da." Cooper was trying to teach him "disintegrate."

Grandma, in that time, had made it through an entire song, from beginning to end, on the flute. Vivaldi it was, she said.

"*My* version of Vivaldi," she added.

Grandfather made several trips to town in the car, alone, giving us all sly looks as he left and sly ones when he returned. He carried packages, and one large box, into the barn.

"Do not follow me!" he commanded in a
loud, serious voice, making Cat and me burst
out laughing and Grandma smile.

"What's he doing?" Cat asked Grandma.

"Secrets," said Grandma. "Secrets even from
me, can you believe that?"

She walked to the entrance of the barn.

"Marcus, darlin' man," she called. "What are
you doing?"

Grandfather's voice came from the back of
the barn.

"Don't sweet talk me, Lottie."

Grandma went back to practicing Vivaldi on
the porch, surrounded by her claque of cats, and
later, when my sister and I went to the barn for
raspberry buckets, there was a shiny new lock
on the door to the toolroom. Grandfather
wasn't in sight, but we heard sounds behind the
door.

Cat knocked.

"Grandfather?"

"I'm busy now." His voice was muffled. "I'm
busy in my office."

His office? Cat mouthed the words to me,

and we grinned at each other and went to pick
black raspberries.

The raspberries grew past the pasture, at the
far edges of the meadow where wild chicory and
Queen Anne's lace grew, too. Grandma had put
a net over them to keep the birds away. Cat and
I pushed back the net and ducked under.

"Every third or every fourth?" Cat asked,
holding a berry to her lips.

"Every other?"

"Third," Cat said, popping the berry into her
mouth.

We picked for a while in silence. The berries
made a soft plunking sound when we dropped
them in the buckets.

"Remember when we used to make tents in
the backyard?" I said, sitting back, looking up
at the sky through the netting.

Cat nodded.

"You liked to build the tents," she said. "And
when you were done you'd sit inside, all restless
and jittery, waiting for something more to happen."

"That's because I loved to build them," I said.

"And I loved to sit inside after you'd gone," said Cat.

There was a silence. Cat reached over to touch my arm.

"What are you thinking about?"

"Something Grandfather said, Mama waiting for things to happen. Remember when Mama got into the tent with us once?"

Cat nodded.

"She sat for a minute, then looked at us and said, 'Well, what happens now?' "

"You and I," I said, "we weren't enough."

I ate a raspberry. It was sour, and for a moment my tongue stung a little.

"Cat."

She looked up.

"I'm sorry. I'm sorry I couldn't put the pictures together. I wanted to make things all right again."

Cat smiled.

"I know. You and Grandfather, two of a kind."

"What do you mean?"

Cat sat back on her heels.

"Why do you think Grandfather takes family pictures?"

"He likes to. He likes the camera."

"No," said Cat. "*You* like the camera in your own way, Journey. Don't you know that Grandfather wants to give you back everything that Mama took away? He wants to give you family."

All those times. All those times that Grandfather had rounded us up, gathered us together for family pictures; plucking us out of hiding places, down from trees and from inside the pantry and from under the bed.

"Things for me to look back on," I whispered.

"Things for him to look back on, too," Cat added.

Cat dropped a berry in the bucket.

"Cat, do you hate Mama?"

Cat stared at the bucket.

"I hate what she did."

I nodded.

"You say that, but do you feel that way?"

Cat looked up.

"I'm trying."

I squeezed a berry between my fingers.

"Do you think she cares about us?"

Cat sighed.

"The only way she can, Journey."

She ate a berry, and the juice made a tiny rivulet down her chin. I peered up suddenly at the sun shining through the net like an out-of-focus picture, then back at Cat. The pattern of the netting sat like a spider web across her face.

"What? What's wrong?" she asked me.

"I wish I had Grandfather's camera right now," I said, beginning to smile.

Cat's eyes widened. I got up quickly, and she scrambled up and after me, chasing me out into the meadow. We startled the redwings, and they flew up above us. A woodchuck on the stone wall ducked away.

Behind us the birds began to eat the raspberries under the net, but it didn't matter.

Chapter Thirteen

It was evening, and the moon hung over the barn. Bloom lay on my bed. Upstairs, over my head in Mama's room, there were footsteps. Bloom looked up and her ears rose. A drawer opened and shut, then another. I looked up, waiting, and in a moment Grandfather stood at my bedroom door.

"Good night, Journey."

He held a large envelope and one of the kittens.

"Are you going to bed now?" I asked.

Grandfather, not speaking, stared over my head at the moon out the window. He had been restless and absentminded all day, drumming his fingers on the table at dinner, pursing his lips thoughtfully. Twice he opened his mouth to say something and didn't. Once, in the middle of our conversation, he said suddenly, "Well, do you think . . . ?" to no one. We had turned to look at him, waiting, but he'd gone back to eating.

"He's cooking up something," Grandma had said at the kitchen sink, handing me a dish to dry. "I would spy on him, or better yet, ask him, but it's too much fun making him wait."

"You mean he wants to tell us what he's doing?"

"Maybe. Maybe he wants to be asked, but you can do that when the time comes."

"When? What time?"

"You'll know," Grandma had said.

Grandfather stood still in my bedroom. The kitten in his arms yawned.

"Grandfather. Grandfather?"

"What? Oh, no, I'm not going to bed yet." He shook his head. "No, I've got work to do."

He put the kitten down and looked at me with a small smile that was more than just a smile.

"Grandfather, were you in Mama's room?"

"Ah, yes. . . ."

I knew the tone. He didn't want to say, or he wouldn't say.

"The kitten had gone in there," he said. "Well, good night."

"Good night."

I heard his footsteps down the hallway and into the kitchen. Then the screen door opened and shut with a small squeak. Out my window I watched him cross the yard and go into the barn, shutting the door behind him. Inside, the barn light went on. Then, as I watched, it went off again.

*   *   *

I am asleep and flying. Cooper and Emmett are there in my dream, and I patiently explain that this is a dream, my flying dream. Cooper smiles at me, and Emmett reaches out a small hand to touch me. "Do you think we could fly, too?" asks Cooper. I am about to say "yes," but I say "wait" instead.

*   *   *

"Wait!" I said out loud.

I sat up in bed, awake. Beside me the kittens stirred. I got out of bed and walked to the window. The moon had gone, but the outside light was on. I turned the lamp on beside my bed. It was four o'clock. Bloom, from her box in the closet, made a small sound in her throat. I turned off the light and went down the hallway, barefoot, and out into the yard.

The moon had set behind the house. I picked my way across the yard, wishing I had thought of shoes. There was dew on the grass and on the stones when I got to the driveway. Very slowly I opened the barn door and slipped inside. I had never been in the barn at night, and there were new shapes and shadows. It did not look like the same place that it was in daylight. It was as if I were still dreaming, as if I had come to a different barn that was like but not like our barn.

I walked past the grain buckets and the wooden bins; somewhere behind the hay there was a rustle, a mouse or a barn rat. I walked past the stalls to the back of the barn. The door

to Grandfather's back room was closed, but a
slice of red light spilled across my bare toes
through the space at the bottom of the door.
Very carefully I turned the knob. Very slowly I
pushed the door open.

The room was filled with the red light, spilling over the table, over equipment, over my
grandfather. There was a sharp, strange smell
in the room. Grandfather bent over a tray
of liquid, staring at something there. Then
he picked up a piece of paper out of the
tray.

Grandfather set Grandma's metronome
going, and it began to click back and forth.
Click. Click. Click. I watched it, half hypnotized
by the sound and the movement. And then, very
slowly, Grandfather turned his head and looked
at me. He looked at my pajamas, then down at
my feet. *Click. Click. Click.*

"Where are your shoes?" he asked, his voice
making me jump.

I opened my mouth to answer him, and then
I saw it. Behind Grandfather, hanging on a line,
held by clothespins, was my family picture. The

picture of the kittens and Bloom in a box, Cooper with his cowboy hat, Cat leaning against Grandmother, and me, lying in Grandfather's arms, my face turned to the camera with a startled look.

"What . . ." I started to speak.

"Don't talk for a minute," said Grandfather, taking what I saw was a picture out of a tray and putting it into another.

He reached up and turned the red light out and the overhead light on. I blinked, then came closer to the table and looked down. It was the picture of Cooper on his bicycle, his mouth open, looking amazed.

"The day I drove the car," I said.

Grandfather smiled at me.

"A darkroom," I said, smiling back at him. "You did this?"

Grandfather, his hair all tousled, grinned wider.

He saw me looking at my family picture.

"That is a fine picture," he said.

"Not perfect," I said. "But . . ."

"Good enough," we said, almost at the same time.

Then Grandfather lifted his shoulders in a sigh, his face slipping out of his grin.

"And there's more, Journey," he said softly.

*   *   *

In the large envelope are the negatives of Mama's pictures. Grandfather spreads them out on the table, and I hold one up to the light, my hand trembling. The people in the picture, all white as if they've been caught in a flash of sun, stare at me. There is a baby.

"This one," I say, my voice a whisper.

Grandfather nods and hands me another. He watches me as I hold it up.

It is a man, a baby on his knees. I stare at it for a moment. Then Grandfather reaches up to turn on the red light.

Grandfather talks softly all the time, his face touched by the glow of the red light, telling me what he's doing. But I hardly hear his words. He tells me about the enlarger and how it works, but silently I wait and watch as, like a face out of the fog, Mama's face appears on the paper,

Papa beside her, the two of them smiling at the baby who is me. The baby's hand reaches out and the mother bends toward him. After the shutter clicks she will kiss him.

I stare at Mama's face. Then at Papa's. And something that I've been trying to remember appears in my mind suddenly, like a face on a piece of paper. My papa's face is a face I don't know. *It is a face I don't remember*.

Grandfather washes the picture and hangs it up to dry. He sucks in his breath with a little whooshing sound.

"Now," he says, "the other picture."

I put my hand on his arm.

"I know," I say. "I already know."

Grandfather is not surprised. He smiles a little and looks up at my family picture.

"I sat on *your* knees," I say, "not on Papa's. And you sang 'Trot, trot to Boston.' It was your shirt, your button I remembered." I pause, then whisper. "It was *your* face."

Grandfather takes down my family picture.

"And this was when you knew," Grandfather says.

I stare at my startled face in the picture as I lay sprawled in Grandfather's lap.

*   *   *

We turn out the lights and walk out into the barn. I trail my fingers along the wood walls. I touch the hay, as if touching it somehow makes it mine.

Grandfather reaches over and takes my hand. At the door I stop suddenly.

"Once they loved me," I say.

His hand tightens around mine, and when we open the door and walk out of the barn, the night has gone, and the sun has come up.